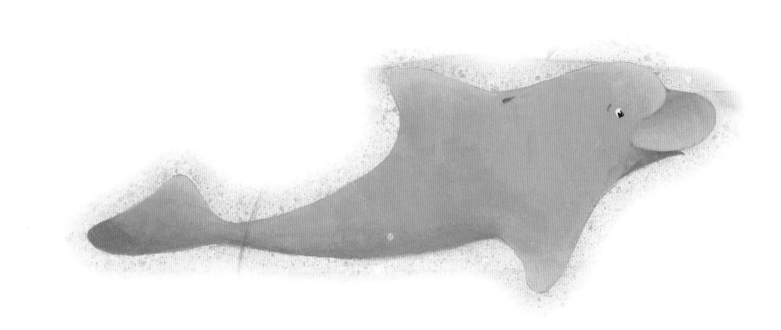

This is a Parragon book
First published in 2006
Parragon, Queen Street House, 4 Queen Street
Bath, BA1 1HE, UK
Copyright © Parragon Books Ltd 2006

ISBN 978-1-4054-7604-1
Printed in China

Dolphin finds a Star

Illustrated by Alex Burnett   Written by Moira Butterfield

One night in the moonlight, a baby dolphin called Splash looked up and saw a shooting star. It zoomed across the sky and disappeared.

"That star has fallen into the water!"
Splash cried. "I would like to find it and
give it to my mommy as a present."

"I can see something shining," said Splash, and he swam toward the sparkles, thinking it was the star.

But when he got closer, he saw that it was a shoal of flashing fish, wiggling and weaving through the water.

Then Splash saw something glowing above his head. "There's the star! My mommy will be so pleased," he thought happily, and he swam toward the shining light.

But when he got closer, Splash found that the light was a lamp shining on the very top of a sail boat.

The more the baby dolphin swam around, the more shiny creatures he saw, swimming and spinning in the water.

There were flashing fish,
jiggly jellyfish, and even sparkly
seahorses, but the fallen star was
nowhere to be found.

At last, Splash saw a light that was much brighter than all the rest. He swam toward it, hoping it would be the star.

He swam through an underwater garden of swirling seaweed and shimmering shells. He even swam past a pile of pirate treasure.

And then, at last, he found the star. It was in the hair of a beautiful mermaid queen sitting on her throne.

"Hello, baby dolphin. What brings you here?" she asked, but Splash felt very shy. He didn't know what to say.

So the flashing fish, the jiggly jellyfish and the sparkly seahorses all told the mermaid queen: "He was looking for the star that's in your hair. He wanted to give it to his mommy."

"In that case, you should have it, because you are very kind," said the mermaid, and she handed the shining star to Splash.

Splash gave his mommy the star, and she was very pleased. Together, they played with it all day long.

Then, when night came, they jumped up as high as they could and pushed it back up into the sky, where it could shine down on everyone - on the flashing fish and the jiggly jellyfish, on the sparkly seahorses and on you, too.